To Alexandra, a loving friend and daughter   KH

To John and Pauline Craig   HC

VIKING/PUFFIN

Published by the Penguin Group
Penguin Books Ltd, 27 Wrights Lane, London W8 5TZ, England
Penguin Books USA Inc., 375 Hudson Street, New York, New York 10014, USA
Penguin Books Australia Ltd, Ringwood, Victoria, Australia
Penguin Books Canada Ltd, 10 Alcorn Avenue, Toronto, Ontario, Canada M4V 3B2
Penguin Books India (P) Ltd, 11 Community Centre, Panchsheel Park, New Delhi – 110 017, India
Penguin Books (NZ) Ltd, Cnr Rosedale and Airborne Roads, Albany, Auckland, New Zealand
Penguin Books (South Africa) (Pty) Ltd, 5 Watkins Street, Denver Ext 4, Johannesburg 2094, South Africa

On the World Wide Web at: www.penguin.com

Penguin Books Ltd, Registered Offices: Harmondsworth, Middlesex, England

First published by Aurum Press Ltd 1987
Published by Viking 2001
1 3 5 7 9 10 8 6 4 2
Published in Puffin Books 2001
1 3 5 7 9 10 8 6 4 2

Copyright © HIT Entertainment plc, 2001
Text copyright © Katharine Holabird, 1987
Illustrations copyright © Helen Craig, 1987

Printed in Italy by Printer Trento Srl

British Library Cataloguing in Publication Data
A CIP catalogue record for this book is available from the British Library

ISBN 0–670–91157–7 Hardback
ISBN 0–140–56867–0 Paperback

To find out more about Angelina, visit her web site at **www.angelinaballerina.com**

Angelina
and Alice

Story by **Katharine Holabird** Illustrations by **Helen Craig**

VIKING

PUFFIN BOOKS

Angelina jumped for joy the day Alice came to school.
Alice loved to dance and do gymnastics, and was
good at all the same things as Angelina. They quickly
became close friends and were always together. At breaks
they skipped rope and did cartwheels round and round
the playground.

They loved to see who could hang upside down longest on the trapeze bar without wiggling, swing highest on the swings, or do the most somersaults in the air.

Angelina was good at cartwheels and could
even do the splits, but Alice could do
a perfect handstand with her toes
pointed straight in the air, and
never lose her balance.

Angelina always fell over when she tried to do a handstand, which was embarrassing, especially on the playground.

One day Angelina fell right on her bottom and the older children pointed at her and laughed. One of them giggled and said, "Look at Angelina Tumbelina!" Another whispered to Alice, and then …

… something awful happened. Alice giggled too, and
ran off to play with the older children while Angelina
sat behind the swings and cried.

The next day was worse. They were all saying, "Angelina Tumbelina!" in the playground, and Angelina couldn't find Alice anywhere. Angelina couldn't concentrate at school and made lots of mistakes in her spelling. She couldn't eat her sandwiches at lunch either, and by the time the class was lining up for sports, Angelina felt so sick she wished she could go home.

Mr Hopper, the sports teacher, blew his whistle for silence and said, "You've all worked so hard at your gymnastics over the year that we are going to do a show for the village festival. Everyone needs to find a partner and start practising now."

Angelina looked at the floor. Who could she ask? She was afraid nobody would be her partner. A big tear rolled down her nose.

Then she felt a tap on her shoulder. It was Alice!
"Will you be my partner, please?" Alice asked.

All that afternoon Angelina and
Alice worked on handstands in the
gymnasium. "Just keep your head
down and line up your tail with the
tip of your nose," Alice said patiently.
"That always helps me to stay up
straight longer." Alice was a good
teacher, and soon Angelina could do
a handstand without falling at all.

Mr Hopper taught them
how to swing in a beautiful
circle over the bar, and how
to actually fly through the
air and land neatly balanced
on the mat.

He taught them to work with the rings and on the bars

and to do rhythmic gymnastics with coloured ribbons.

Finally, Mr Hopper showed them a
terrific balancing trick they could
do for the show.

The day of the village festival was
bright and beautiful.

TODAY
A DISPLAY
OF
GYMNASTICS
BY THE
CHILDREN
OF
MOUSE SCHOOL

The gymnastics class did a wonderful display at the village festival with high jumps, back flips, and balancing on the bars. When Angelina and Alice did their balancing act together even the older children were impressed. "Wow!" they said. "How did you learn to do those amazing tricks?"

PIN THE TAIL ON THE CAT & WIN A PRIZE!

After the show, Mr Hopper smiled and said, "That was really good teamwork!" Alice and Angelina grinned back. "That's because we're such good friends," they said together.

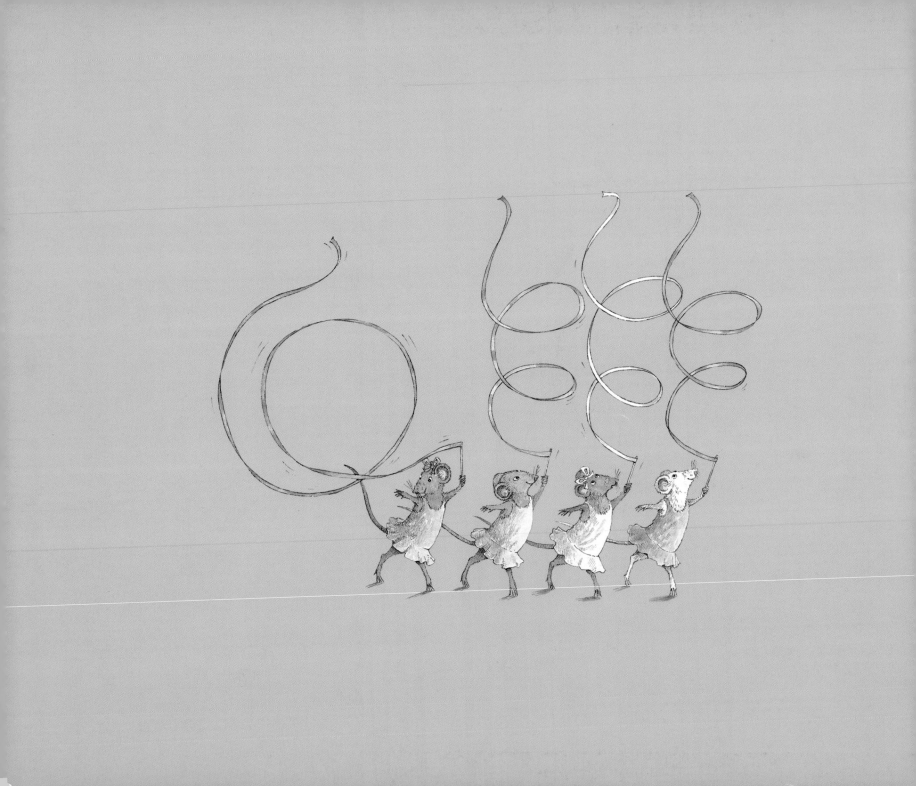